# Frankenstein

## THE GRAPHIC NOVEL
### Mary Shelley

## QUICK TEXT VERSION

Script Adaptation: Jason Cobley
Linework: Declan Shalvey
Colouring: Jason Cardy & Kat Nicholson
Lettering: Terry Wiley
Art Director: Jon Haward
Design & Layout: Jo Wheeler & Jenny Placentino
Publishing Assistant: Joanna Watts
Additional Information: Karen Wenborn

Editor in Chief: Clive Bryant

Frankenstein: The Graphic Novel
Quick Text Version

Mary Shelley

First UK Edition

Published by: Classical Comics Ltd

All enquiries should be addressed to:
Classical Comics Ltd.
PO Box 7280
Litchborough
Towcester
NN12 9AR
United Kingdom
Tel: 0845 812 3000

info@classicalcomics.com
www.classicalcomics.com

ISBN: 978-1-906332-16-7

Printed in the UK

This book is printed in the UK by Red Fox Ltd using biodegradable vegetable inks, on environmentally
friendly paper which is FSC (Forest Stewardship Council) certified (TT-COC-2200) and manufactured to
the accredited Environmental Management Standard ISO 14001. This material can be disposed of by
recycling, incineration for energy recovery, composting and biodegradation.

Jason Cardy and Kat Nicholson would like to thank Kate Derrick and
Dylan Cook for their help with preparing the pages for colouring.
The publishers would like to acknowledge the design assistance of
Greg Powell in the completion of this book.

The rights of Jason Cobley, Declan Shalvey, Jason Cardy, Kat Nicholson, Terry Wiley and Jon Howard
to be identified as the Artists of this work have been asserted in accordance with the
Copyright, Designs and Patents Act 1988 sections 77 and 78.

# Contents

# Dramatis Personæ

Victor Frankenstein

Frankenstein's Monster

Elizabeth Lavenza
*Victor's adopted sister*

Robert Walton
*Adventurer*

The Ship's Master

The Ship's Lieutenant

Alphonse Frankenstein
*Victor's father*

Caroline Frankenstein
*Victor's mother*

Ernest Frankenstein
*Victor's brother*

William Frankenstein
*Victor's brother*

Henry Clerval
*Victor's friend*

Justine Moritz
*Servant to Frankenstein's household*

# Dramatis Personæ

**Monsieur Krempe**
*Professor of Natural Philosophy,*
*University of Ingolstadt*

**Monsieur Waldman**
*Professor of Chemistry,*
*University of Ingolstadt*

**Lawyer**
*States the charge against*
*Justine Moritz*

**Old Woman**
*Gives evidence against*
*Justine Mortiz*

**Monsieur DeLacy**
*Cottage Dweller*

**Agatha DeLacy**
*Daughter of*
*Monsieur DeLacy*

**Felix DeLacy**
*Son of Monsieur DeLacy*

**Turkish Merchant**

**Safie**
*Daughter of the Turkish Merchant*

**Mr Kirwin**
*Magistrate*

**Fisherman**

**Genevan Judge**

# Prologue

Mary Shelley's literary masterpiece *Frankenstein* was unleashed upon the world in 1818. It was written before the days of steam travel, when the world seemed a much larger place than it does today. Far-off places were out of the reach of all but the bravest adventurers; and in those unknown places it was possible that things could exist — even things created by man himself — that would terrify anyone who saw them.

Science was progressing at an astounding pace. It seemed that anything and everything was possible, as the human race found new and more powerful ways to create, and also to destroy.

At the same time, medical science was finding new ways to heal the sick and to revive the dying; and it started to raise questions about the nature of life itself. If the dying can be revived, then could the dead also be brought back to life? How about a dead person that had been assembled from the parts of other dead people? Could that be given life too?

Where would it all end? Would this all go too far? And if so, what would the consequences be?

**Indeed, in this early world of advancing medical science, anything and everything seemed possible.......**

**LETTER I - DECEMBER 11TH**

MY DEAR **SISTER...**

I AM **ALREADY** FAR **NORTH** OF **LONDON.**

THE **NORTH POLE** IS A **LAND** FULL OF **WONDERS** AND **BEAUTY,** WHERE THE **SUN** NEVER **SETS.**

FOR AS LONG AS I CAN **REMEMBER**, THIS **JOURNEY** HAS BEEN MY **DREAM**.

I **DESERVE** TO DO SOMETHING **GREAT**!

LETTER II - MARCH 28TH

TIME PASSES SO **SLOWLY** HERE, MARGARET, AND I AM **LONELY**.

LETTER III - JULY 7TH

WE ARE **FAR**, FAR NORTH NOW; BUT I WILL BE **CAREFUL**.

LETTER IV - AUGUST 5TH

LAST **MONDAY,** OUR **SHIP** WAS SURROUNDED BY ICE AND **FOG.**

WHEN THE **FOG** FINALLY **CLEARED,** WE SAW A **STRANGE SIGHT.**

IT WAS A **HUGE MAN,** A **DISTANCE AWAY** FROM US. WE WERE **STUCK** IN THE **ICE,** SO WE **COULDN'T FOLLOW HIM.**

IN THE **MORNING**, THE **SAILORS** WERE TALKING TO **SOMEONE OVERBOARD** - IT WAS A **MAN** STRANDED IN THE **ICY COLD**.

OUR **CAPTAIN** WILL **LOOK AFTER** YOU.

PLEASE **TELL ME** WHERE YOUR **SHIP** IS HEADED.

THE **NORTH POLE**.

HE **AGREED** TO COME **ON BOARD**.

I NEVER **SAW** A MAN IN SUCH A **DREADFUL STATE**. **SLOWLY**, WE HELPED HIM TO **RECOVER**. IT WAS **TWO DAYS** BEFORE HE COULD **SPEAK**.

FOR SEVERAL YEARS, I WAS THEIR *ONLY CHILD.* THEY *TRULY LOVED* ME.

WHEN I WAS *FIVE YEARS OLD,* MY *MOTHER* ADOPTED THE *ORPHANED DAUGHTER* OF A *NOBLEMAN.*

*ELIZABETH LAVENZA* BECAME *MORE* THAN JUST A *SISTER* TO ME - FOR I TRULY *ADORED HER.*

VOLUME I
CHAPTER II

THERE WAS *LESS* THAN A *YEAR BETWEEN US.*

MY *PARENTS* SETTLED IN *GENEVA* WHEN THEIR *SECOND SON* WAS BORN...

...THERE, I BECAME *GREAT FRIENDS* WITH *HENRY CLERVAL.* HE LOVED TO *READ* AND *WRITE,* AS WELL AS *ACT.*

ELIZABETH WAS LOVELY, AND BROUGHT OUT THE BEST IN ALL OF US.

I STUDIED THE WORKS OF GREAT THINKERS.

HERE WERE MEN WHO HAD DISCOVERED THE SECRETS OF NATURE.

AND WHAT GLORY WOULD BE MINE, IF I COULD RID MAN OF ILLNESS!

WHEN I WAS FIFTEEN, WE SAW A TERRIBLE THUNDERSTORM.

THE NEXT **MORNING**, WE FOUND THE **TREE** SHATTERED INTO **THIN RIBBONS** OF **WOOD**. AT **ONCE** I BEGAN TO **STUDY** THE **MATHEMATICS** AND **SCIENCE** OF **ELECTRICITY**.

BUT **DESTINY** HAD ALREADY **DECIDED** ON MY **DESTRUCTION**.

VOLUME I
CHAPTER III

WHEN I WAS **SEVENTEEN**, I WAS DUE TO **LEAVE** FOR INGOLSTADT UNIVERSITY...

...BUT **ELIZABETH** CAUGHT **SCARLET FEVER**. SHE RECOVERED, BUT MY **MOTHER** BECAME **SICK** FROM **TENDING** TO HER.

My **children**, your **marriage** together would make me very **happy**.

Elizabeth, you must be a **mother** to my younger children.

I hope to **see** you in **another** world...

SHE DIED *CALMLY.*

MY MOTHER WAS *DEAD...*

...BUT WE *STILL* HAD *DUTIES* TO PERFORM. ELIZABETH LOOKED AFTER US, AND GAVE *COMFORT.*

FINALLY, THE *DAY* CAME FOR ME TO *LEAVE* FOR INGOLSTADT.

WRITE *OFTEN,* VICTOR.

I *LOVED* MY *FAMILY,* ELIZABETH AND CLERVAL; BUT I *LONGED* TO *ACQUIRE KNOWLEDGE.*

17

MONSIEUR *WALDMAN* AND I BECAME *FRIENDS.*

*TWO YEARS* PASSED, AND WITH HIS *HELP,* I MADE *DISCOVERIES* THAT BUILT MY *REPUTATION* AT THE *UNIVERSITY.*

I WAS *INTERESTED* IN ANYTHING THAT *LIVED.* MOST OF *ALL,* I WANTED TO KNOW HOW *LIFE* WAS *CREATED.*

TO UNDERSTAND *LIFE,* WE MUST *FIRST* UNDERSTAND *DEATH.*

TO *ME,* A *CHURCHYARD* WAS JUST A PLACE FULL OF *DEAD BODIES* THAT HAD BECOME *FOOD* FOR *WORMS.*

I SPENT *DAYS* AND *NIGHTS* EXAMINING *DEAD BODIES.* I *SAW* HOW MAN *DECAYED* AND I *EXAMINED* EVERY LITTLE *DETAIL...*

*...UNTIL,* AFTER *WEEKS* OF *WORK,* I DISCOVERED...

...THE *SECRET* OF *LIFE!*

I KNEW HOW TO GIVE *LIFE* TO *LIFELESS* MATTER.

YET TO *PREPARE* THE *BODY* FOR IT WITH *FIBRES, MUSCLES* AND *VEINS* SEEMED *IMPOSSIBLE.*

I DECIDED TO MAKE THE BODY *LARGER* SO THAT IT WAS *EASIER* TO *PUT TOGETHER.*

IN A *SOLITARY* ROOM I WORKED ON MY *CREATION.*

SO *DETERMINED* WAS I, THAT I MADE MYSELF *ILL.* I DIDN'T *STOP* WORKING, EVEN TO *LOOK AFTER* MYSELF.

21

ON A *DREARY NIGHT* IN *NOVEMBER,* I FINALLY FINISHED.

CHINKK!

SMASH!

I COULDN'T **BEAR** TO **SEE** HIM.

I **RAN** OUT OF THE **ROOM**.

CRASH!

I **THREW** MYSELF ONTO MY BED TO TRY TO **REST** - BUT I **COULDN'T** GET THE **MONSTER** OUT OF MY **MIND**...

...AND MY **SLEEP** WAS **BROKEN** BY TERRIBLE DREAMS.

I DREAMT OF ELIZABETH, WALKING IN INGOLSTADT.

I EMBRACED HER...

...BUT AS WE KISSED...

...SHE TURNED THE COLOUR OF DEATH...

WHEN **MORNING** CAME, I **WALKED** THE STREETS OF **INGOLSTADT**, FEARING THE **MONSTER** EVERYWHERE I **WENT**.

I WAS **TOO SCARED** TO RETURN TO MY **APARTMENT**.

I DIDN'T REALLY KNOW **WHERE I WAS** OR **WHAT I WAS DOING**.

MY **HEART POUNDED** WITH **FEAR**.

MY **DEAR FRANKENSTEIN!**

I'M SO **GLAD** TO **SEE YOU!**

I TREMBLED AS WE WALKED TO MY COLLEGE.

I WAS AFRAID TO MEET WITH THE CREATURE IN MY APARTMENT...

...BUT EVEN MORE SCARED THAT HENRY SHOULD SEE HIM.

PLEASE WAIT HERE.

I CHECKED THAT MY ENEMY WASN'T THERE.

I CLAPPED MY HANDS WITH JOY AND RAN DOWN FOR HENRY.

I WAS *TOO* EXCITED TO EAT.

HA-HA HA HA-HAH!!!

HA-HARRH!

VICTOR! WHAT ON *EARTH* IS THE MATTER?

HA HA HA HA!

WHAT'S *CAUSING* YOU TO *BE* LIKE THIS?

I THOUGHT I SAW THE *MONSTER* IN MY *ROOM*...

DON'T *ASK*...

...*HE* CAN TELL *YOU!*

DEAR VICTOR,

YOU HAVE BEEN **VERY ILL**, AND DESPITE **HENRY'S LETTERS**, I'VE BEEN SO **WORRIED**.

GET **WELL** AND COME **HOME** - YOUR **FATHER** WOULD BE **SO HAPPY** TO **SEE** YOU.

**ERNEST** IS NOW **SIXTEEN** AND WANTS TO WORK **AWAY** FROM **HOME** - BUT WE WANT **YOU** BACK HERE BEFORE WE LET HIM **GO**.

I WISH YOU COULD SEE LOVELY LITTLE **WILLIAM**. HE IS SO **FULL** OF **CHARACTER** AND HAS **ALREADY** HAD **TWO GIRLFRIENDS!**

DO YOU REMEMBER OUR SERVANT, **JUSTINE MORITZ?** HER **MOTHER** TREATED HER **BADLY**, AND SHE CAME TO **LIVE** WITH US WHEN SHE WAS **TWELVE**.

YOU MAY **REMEMBER**, SHE WAS A **GREAT FAVOURITE** OF YOURS.

**ONE** BY **ONE**, HER BROTHERS AND SISTER **DIED**, AND **JUSTINE** WAS CALLED BACK **HOME**. HER **MOTHER** WOULD SOMETIMES **BEG** FOR JUSTINE'S **FORGIVENESS**, AND THEN **BLAME HER** FOR CAUSING THE **DEATHS** OF HER **BROTHERS** AND SISTER.

BUT JUSTINE'S **MOTHER** IS AT **PEACE** NOW; SHE **DIED** AT THE START OF **WINTER**.

**JUSTINE** HAS **RETURNED** TO US, AND I **LOVE** HER **DEARLY**.

I FEEL **BETTER** FOR WRITING THIS **LETTER** TO YOU. **TAKE CARE** OF YOURSELF, AND **PLEASE WRITE**!

*ELIZABETH*

DEAR **ELIZABETH**! I WILL **WRITE** IMMEDIATELY!

I BEGAN TO **RECOVER**. TWO WEEKS LATER, I WAS **WELL** ENOUGH TO **LEAVE** MY **ROOM**.

I COULD NEVER TELL *HENRY* ABOUT WHAT I'D *DONE*, OR WHAT *HAPPENED* ON THAT *TERRIBLE NIGHT.*

*CLERVAL* CAME TO THE *UNIVERSITY* TO STUDY *ORIENTAL LANGUAGES*, AND I STUDIED *WITH* HIM.

I FOUND *PEACE* IN THE WORKS OF THE *ORIENTALISTS.*

LIFE SEEMS LIKE *SUNSHINE* AND *ROSES* WHEN YOU READ THEIR *WRITINGS!*

SUMMER PASSED, AND WITH THE ARRIVAL OF WINTER AND SNOW, MY RETURN TO GENEVA WAS DELAYED UNTIL THE FOLLOWING SPRING.

CLERVAL SUGGESTED WE TAKE A FAREWELL TOUR OF INGOLSTADT.

WHAT A TRUE FRIEND!

OVER THOSE TWO WEEKS, HE TAUGHT ME TO LOVE NATURE AGAIN, AND TO ENJOY THE CHEERFUL FACES OF CHILDREN.

FOR THE FIRST TIME IN YEARS, I BECAME HAPPY AGAIN.

BLAC

I RETURNED TO FIND A LETTER FROM MY FATHER:

DEAR VICTOR,

YOU ARE PROBABLY KEEN TO COME HOME TO US, SO HOW CAN I TELL YOU THIS?

WILLIAM, OUR SWEET, GENTLE CHILD, HAS BEEN MURDERED!

LAST THURSDAY, WE ALL WENT FOR A WALK IN PLAINPALAIS...

ONLY *YOU* CAN COMFORT ELIZABETH. SHE WEEPS *CONSTANTLY* AND BLAMES *HERSELF* FOR WILLIAM'S DEATH.

*PLEASE* COME *HOME* TO US, VICTOR.

YOUR *FATHER,*

ALPHONSE FRANKENSTEIN.

MY DEAR *FRANKENSTEIN,* WHAT ARE YOU GOING TO *DO?*

I'LL GO TO GENEVA, IMMEDIATELY.

I SAID *GOODBYE* TO MY *FRIEND,* AND AS I GOT *CLOSER* TO *HOME,* I WAS *OVERCOME* WITH *GRIEF* AND *FEAR.*

ALTHOUGH IT WAS **DARK** WHEN I REACHED **GENEVA**, I WAS UNABLE TO **REST**.

I DECIDED TO **VISIT** THE SPOT WHERE **WILLIAM** WAS **MURDERED**, AND HAD TO TRAVEL BY **BOAT** TO GET THERE.

**LIGHTNING** FLASHED TOWARDS US, AND **THUNDER** CRASHED **OVERHEAD**.

KRAKKA-DOOM!

WILLIAM, DEAR **ANGEL**!

**THIS** IS YOUR **FUNERAL**!

AS I *SAID* THESE *WORDS*, I SAW A *FIGURE* IN THE *GLOOM*.

A FLASH OF *LIGHTNING* REVEALED THAT IT WAS *THE WRETCH*...

...THE *FILTHY DEMON* I HAD *GIVEN LIFE* TO.

WHAT WAS HE *DOING* THERE? COULD *HE* BE THE *MURDERER* OF MY *BROTHER*?

NOTHING *HUMAN* COULD HAVE *HARMED* THAT *FAIR CHILD*.

HE WAS THE *MURDERER!*

I COULDN'T *FOLLOW* HIM - HE *DISAPPEARED* AMONG THE *ROCKS* OF *MOUNT SALÊVE*.

44

HE SOON REACHED THE *SUMMIT*...

...AND *DISAPPEARED*.

PAPA! VICTOR SAYS THAT *JUSTINE* IS *INNOCENT!*

IF SHE *IS*, THEN *GOD FORBID* THAT SHE IS FOUND *GUILTY.*

DEAR COUSIN, YOU FILL ME WITH *HOPE.* I'LL *NEVER* BE HAPPY *AGAIN* IF JUSTINE IS *CONDEMNED.*

DON'T WORRY - THE *COURT* SHALL *PROVE* THAT SHE IS *INNOCENT.*

VOLUME I
CHAPTER VIII

A *THOUSAND TIMES* I THOUGHT ABOUT *CONFESSING* TO THE *CRIME* - BUT THEY'D HAVE *THOUGHT* THAT I WAS A *MADMAN.*

JUSTINE SEEMED *CALM* AND *CONFIDENT* IN HER *INNOCENCE* AS SHE ENTERED THE *COURT.*

A *TEAR* CAME INTO HER *EYE* WHEN SHE SAW US.

JUSTINE HAD BEEN **OUT** ON THE **NIGHT** OF THE **MURDER**, AND EARLY IN THE **MORNING** SHE WAS **SEEN** BY A **MARKET-WOMAN**, CLOSE TO WHERE WILLIAM'S **BODY** WAS FOUND.

JUSTINE WAS **CALLED** TO **DEFEND** HERSELF. SHE WAS CLOSE TO **TEARS**, AND HER **VOICE** WAS **SHAKY**.

I ASKED HER WHAT SHE WAS **DOING**, BUT SHE SEEMED **CONFUSED**.

I AM **INNOCENT**.

I SPENT THE EVENING AT MY **AUNT'S HOUSE**. ON THE WAY **BACK**, A **MAN** ASKED ME IF I HAD SEEN THE **CHILD** WHO WAS **LOST**.

I SPENT **MANY HOURS** LOOKING FOR HIM.

I **TRIED** TO RETURN TO **GENEVA**, BUT IT WAS SO **LATE** THAT THE **GATES** WERE **SHUT** --

-- SO I SPENT THE **REST** OF THE NIGHT IN A **BARN**.

THIS **PICTURE** WAS FOUND IN **JUSTINE'S POCKET**.

IT'S THE **SAME ONE** THAT **WILLIAM** WAS WEARING BEFORE HE WENT **MISSING**.

AT **DAWN**, I WAS **WOKEN** BY THE SOUND OF **FOOTSTEPS**. I DECIDED TO **LOOK** FOR THE **MISSING CHILD** AGAIN.

I WAS STILL **WEARY** FROM HAVING HAD **LITTLE SLEEP** WHEN I MET WITH THE **MARKET-WOMAN**.

I DON'T KNOW **HOW** THE **PICTURE** GOT INTO MY **POCKET**. I **KNOW** HOW **BAD** THAT LOOKS FOR ME, BUT I **CANNOT EXPLAIN** IT.

IT'S UP TO THE **COURT** TO **DECIDE** WHAT HAPPENS TO ME **NOW**.

A **MURMUR** OF **HORROR** FILLED THE **COURT**.

SEVERAL **WITNESSES** WERE CALLED TO HER **DEFENCE**, AND **ELIZABETH** EVEN SPOKE TO THE COURT **DIRECTLY**, BUT **OPINION** WENT **AGAINST JUSTINE**.

IN THE MORNING, I WENT TO THE **COURT** TO HEAR THE **VERDICT**: **JUSTINE** WAS FOUND **GUILTY**.

...BUT SHE HAS **CONFESSED!**

**HOW** CAN I **TRUST** ANYONE **AGAIN?**

I'LL **SEE** HER, **EVEN** THOUGH SHE'S **GUILTY**.

OH, **JUSTINE!** **WHY** DID YOU **DO IT??**

I **THOUGHT** YOU WERE **INNOCENT!**

I **DID** CONFESS, BUT **THAT** WAS A **LIE!** I **AM** INNOCENT!

EVER SINCE I **CAME** HERE, I'VE BEEN **THREATENED** AND **MENACED**, UNTIL I **ALMOST** BEGAN TO THINK THAT I **WAS** THE **MURDERING MONSTER**.

WHAT ELSE COULD I **DO?**

OH, **JUSTINE!** FORGIVE ME FOR NOT **TRUSTING** YOU. DO NOT **FEAR** - I WILL **PROVE** YOUR **INNOCENCE**.

YOU **SHALL** NOT DIE!

I'M NOT **AFRAID** OF DYING;

I CAN **GO** IN **PEACE**, KNOWING THAT YOU **BOTH** BELIEVE I'M INNOCENT.

THE POOR **SUFFERER** TRIED TO COMFORT US **ALL** - BUT **I**, THE **TRUE** MURDERER, FELT **NO CONSOLATION** IN MY **HEART**...

...AND IN THE MORNING, JUSTINE DIED.

I SAW THOSE I LOVED CRYING OVER THE GRAVES OF WILLIAM AND JUSTINE - THE FIRST VICTIMS OF MY CREATION.

## VOLUME II
## CHAPTER I

I HAD STARTED OFF WITH GOOD INTENTIONS, TO BENEFIT MY FELLOW BEINGS. NOW ALL WAS RUINED. FULL OF GUILT, I NEEDED TO BE ALONE.

I HAD BROUGHT ABOUT TERRIBLE EVILS, AND I LIVED IN FEAR OF THE MONSTER STRIKING AGAIN.

WHEN I THINK ABOUT THE MISERABLE DEATH OF JUSTINE, I FEEL AS IF I'M STANDING ON THE EDGE OF A CLIFF, WITH THOUSANDS OF PEOPLE WAITING TO PUSH ME OFF.

WILLIAM AND JUSTINE WERE KILLED, AND THE MURDERER WALKS ABOUT THE WORLD FREE.

WITH MY FATHER'S HEALTH SHAKEN, AND ELIZABETH SO SAD, I COULDN'T COPE ANYMORE; MY SOUL DROVE ME TO SUDDENLY LEAVE.

TRYING TO *FORGET* MY *SORROWS*, I HEADED FOR THE *ALPINE VALLEYS*.

VOLUME II
CHAPTER II

I DECIDED TO *CLIMB* TO THE *SUMMIT* OF *MONTANVERT*.

SEEING THE *GLACIER* THERE HAD A *GREAT EFFECT* ON ME WHEN I FIRST *SAW* IT, *YEARS* AGO.

THE *CLIMB* WAS *HAZARDOUS*, AND MY *SURROUNDINGS* WERE OFTEN *GLOOMY* - BUT *THAT* DIDN'T *STOP* ME.

IT WAS NEARLY **NOON** WHEN I **ARRIVED** AT THE **TOP OF** THE **MOUNTAIN.** I **GAZED** AT THE **WONDERFUL VIEW.**

MY **HEART** SWELLED WITH **JOY.**

WANDERING SPIRITS, ALLOW ME THIS **HAPPINESS,** OR **TAKE ME AWAY** FROM THE **JOYS** OF **LIFE!**

AS I **SPOKE,** I **SUDDENLY SAW** THE **FIGURE** OF A **HUGE MAN** COMING **TOWARDS** ME AT **SUPERHUMAN SPEED.**

IT WAS THE **WRETCH** THAT I HAD **CREATED.** I **SHOOK** WITH **ANGER** AND **HORROR;** WAITING TO **FIGHT** HIM IN **MORTAL COMBAT!**

55

I DECIDED TO LISTEN TO HIS *TALE.*

FOR THE *FIRST TIME,* I *REALISED* THAT, AS *CREATOR* OF THIS *CREATURE,* I HAD *DUTIES* TOWARDS HIM.

VOLUME II
CHAPTER III

I STRUGGLE TO REMEMBER MY *FIRST DAYS* – IT TOOK A WHILE FOR ME TO RECOGNISE MY *SENSES.*

I WENT TO THE *FOREST* NEAR INGOLSTADT. THERE I FOUND BERRIES TO EAT, AND WATER TO DRINK.

I WAS *COLD* AND *FRIGHTENED.* I TOOK SOME OF YOUR *CLOTHES* WHEN I LEFT YOUR *APARTMENT,* BUT THESE *WEREN'T ENOUGH* TO KEEP ME *WARM.* FEELING PAIN, I SAT *DOWN* AND *WEPT.*

OVER THE DAYS, I LEARNT TO *UNDERSTAND* MY *SENSES.*

I TRIED TO IMITATE THE *SOUNDS* OF THE *BIRDS,* BUT THE *NOISES* I MADE FRIGHTENED ME BACK INTO SILENCE.

FOOD WAS SCARCE, AND I OFTEN SPENT THE WHOLE DAY SEARCHING FOR A FEW ACORNS.

I LONGED FOR FOOD AND SHELTER – THEN, I FOUND A SMALL HUT.

THE DOOR WAS OPEN. INSIDE, AN OLD MAN WAS PREPARING HIS BREAKFAST.

HE SAW ME AND RAN AWAY, SCREAMING.

I WAS SURPRISED BY HIS REACTION – BUT I WAS FASCINATED BY THE HUT: HERE WAS A PLACE WHERE THE SNOW AND RAIN COULDN'T GET IN.

I GREEDILY ATE HIS BREAKFAST AND FELL ASLEEP IN THE STRAW.

IT WAS *NOON* WHEN I AWOKE. DRAWN BY THE WARMTH OF THE SUN, I CONTINUED MY JOURNEY.

SEVERAL HOURS LATER, I ARRIVED AT A *VILLAGE.*

AS I ENTERED ONE OF THE *COTTAGES,* THE *CHILDREN* THERE SCREAMED AND A *WOMAN FAINTED.*

THE WHOLE VILLAGE TURNED OUT AGAINST ME, AND ATTACKED ME WITH STONES AND WEAPONS UNTIL I ESCAPED TO THE OPEN COUNTRY.

I TOOK REFUGE IN A SMALL HOVEL. IT WAS NEXT TO A PLEASANT COTTAGE, BUT AFTER WHAT HAPPENED IN THE VILLAGE, I DARED NOT ENTER THAT.

I WAS HAPPY TO HAVE FOUND SHELTER FROM THE WEATHER AND FROM THE CRUELTY OF MAN.

I DRANK WATER FROM THE STREAM AND ATE ANYTHING THAT I COULD FIND OR STEAL.

HIDDEN AWAY, I WATCHED THE PEOPLE THAT LIVED IN THE COTTAGE - AN OLD MAN, A GENTLE GIRL, AND A SAD YOUNG MAN.

THEY SHOWED SUCH KINDNESS AND LOVE FOR EACH OTHER THAT IT MADE ME FEEL NEW EMOTIONS, MYSELF.

ALTHOUGH IT WAS NIGHT, I FOUND THAT THEY COULD EXTEND THE LIGHT BY USING CANDLES...

...WHICH MEANT THAT THE SETTING OF THE SUN DIDN'T PUT AN END TO MY PLEASURE OF WATCHING MY HUMAN NEIGHBOURS.

VOLUME II
CHAPTER IV

I SOON REALISED THAT THE OLD MAN WAS BLIND. THE YOUNG PEOPLE SHOWED MUCH LOVE FOR HIM.

I LONGED TO JOIN THEM, BUT I DARED NOT.

THEY WERE NOT ENTIRELY HAPPY, ALTHOUGH I COULDN'T SEE WHAT MADE THEM SO MISERABLE.

A WHILE LATER, I DISCOVERED ONE OF THE CAUSES: POVERTY.

THEY OFTEN WENT HUNGRY, ESPECIALLY THE YOUNGER COTTAGERS WHO OFTEN PLACED FOOD BEFORE THE OLD MAN AND HAD NONE THEMSELVES.

WHEN I REALISED THIS, I STOPPED TAKING THEIR FOOD AND SATISFIED MYSELF WITH BERRIES, NUTS AND ROOTS FROM THE NEARBY WOOD.

I ALSO LEARNT HOW TO USE THEIR TOOLS SO THAT I COULD HELP THEM WITH THEIR TASKS.

AT NIGHT I WOULD OFTEN BRING FIREWOOD FOR THEM - ENOUGH FOR SEVERAL DAYS.

I DISCOVERED THAT THE WORDS THEY SPOKE TO EACH OTHER WERE IMPORTANT - AND, SLOWLY, I WORKED OUT THE NAMES THAT THEY GAVE TO FAMILIAR OBJECTS.

I LEARNT SIMPLE WORDS, AS WELL AS THE NAMES OF THE COTTAGERS THEMSELVES.

THE OLD MAN WAS "FATHER".

THE GIRL WAS "SISTER", OR "AGATHA".

THE YOUNG MAN WAS "FELIX" "BROTHER", OR "SON".

I WAS SO HAPPY WHEN I DISCOVERED WHAT THESE SOUNDS MEANT, AND WAS ABLE TO SAY THEM. I MADE OUT OTHER WORDS, TOO - LIKE "GOOD", "DEAREST" AND "UNHAPPY".

ALL WINTER I STUDIED THE COTTAGERS TO LEARN THEIR WAYS. I SHARED THEIR JOYS AND THEIR SORROWS.

FELIX WAS THE SADDEST OF THE THREE.

EVEN IN SUCH POVERTY, I SAW HIM BRING HAPPINESS TO HIS SISTER WITH THE GIFT OF A WHITE FLOWER TAKEN FROM THE SNOWY GROUND.

THE COTTAGERS WERE SO BEAUTIFUL, AND I WAS SHOCKED AND TERRIFIED TO SEE HOW UGLY I WAS WHEN I SAW MY REFLECTION IN A POOL.

I DIDN'T BELIEVE IT AT FIRST - BUT I SOON REALISED THAT I WAS TRULY A MONSTER!

EACH DAY WAS MUCH LIKE ANOTHER.

I SLEPT DURING THE DAY AND WORKED FOR THE COTTAGERS ONCE THEY HAD GONE TO SLEEP. I WOULD CLEAR THEIR PATH OF SNOW, AND COLLECT FOOD AND FUEL FOR THEM. THEY THOUGHT IT WAS A "GOOD SPIRIT" THAT DID SUCH WORK FOR THEM, BECAUSE THEY NEVER SAW ME.

I THOUGHT THAT I COULD MAKE THEM HAPPY, AND WIN THEIR FAVOUR. TO DO THIS, I NEEDED TO LEARN THEIR LANGUAGE.

FELIX?

MY *SWEET ARABIAN!*

SPRING CAME, AND YET *FELIX* WAS SADDER THAN EVER.

THEN, HE HAD A *VISITOR.*

THIS *VISITOR* MADE *FELIX* SO VERY HAPPY.

SHE DIDN'T SEEM TO *UNDERSTAND* HIM, BUT *SMILED* A LOT. THEY CALLED HER *"SAFIE".*

JOY SEEMED TO TAKE THE PLACE OF SADNESS. I WATCHED AND *LISTENED* CLOSELY AS *FELIX* TAUGHT SAFIE THEIR *LANGUAGE.*

WE IMPROVED *RAPIDLY,* AND IN THE SPACE OF *TWO MONTHS* I COULD *UNDERSTAND* MOST OF THEIR *WORDS.*

I ALSO *LISTENED* AS THEY STUDIED *BOOKS,* SUCH AS *'RUINS OF EMPIRES',* WHICH SHOWED ME THE *MANNERS, GOVERNMENTS* AND *RELIGIONS* OF *DIFFERENT* COUNTRIES.

WAS MANKIND SO POWERFUL, AND YET AT THE SAME TIME, SO TERRIBLE? TO HEAR OF ALL THE BLOODSHED MADE ME TURN AWAY WITH DISGUST.

AND WHAT WAS I?

I KNEW NOTHING OF MY CREATION OR OF MY CREATOR. I WAS UGLY; AND NOT EVEN OF THE SAME MAKING AS MAN.

WHO WERE THIS FAMILY?

THE DE LACEYS - FROM PARIS.

THEY CAME FROM A GOOD FRENCH FAMILY, WHICH HAD BEEN RUINED BY SAFIE'S FATHER.

HE WAS A TURKISH MERCHANT WHO WAS THROWN INTO PRISON BY THE FRENCH GOVERNMENT AND CONDEMNED TO DEATH.

FELIX, WHO HAD BEEN PRESENT AT THE TRIAL, PROMISED TO FREE HIM...

...AND WHEN HE SAW THE MERCHANT'S BEAUTIFUL DAUGHTER, HE AGREED WITH THE TURK THAT SAFIE SHOULD BE HIS REWARD.

FELIX LED THE FUGITIVES THROUGH FRANCE. SECRETLY, THE TURK HATED THE IDEA OF HIS DAUGHTER MARRYING A CHRISTIAN, AND SO HE HATCHED A PLAN TO DECEIVE FELIX AND TO TAKE HIS DAUGHTER WITH HIM.

FELIX'S PLOT WAS SOON DISCOVERED, AND HIS FATHER AND SISTER WERE THROWN INTO PRISON.

FELIX TURNED HIMSELF IN, SO THAT DE LACY AND AGATHA WOULD BE FREED. HE FAILED.

NEWS OF THIS REACHED FELIX, WHO MADE ARRANGEMENTS WITH THE TURK FOR SAFIE, AND RETURNED QUICKLY TO PARIS.

THEY WERE ALL IMPRISONED FOR FIVE MONTHS, AFTER WHICH THEY WERE STRIPPED OF THEIR FORTUNE, AND SENT AWAY FROM FRANCE FOREVER.

HEARING THAT FELIX HAD LOST HIS FORTUNE, THE TURK TOLD HIS DAUGHTER TO STOP ALL THOUGHTS OF HER LOVER. SAFIE WAS OUTRAGED.

HER FATHER LEFT FOR TURKEY, LEAVING SAFIE ALONE. FINDING SOME PAPERS OF HER FATHER, SHE FOUND OUT THAT FELIX NOW LIVED IN GERMANY - AND SHE DECIDED TO GO THERE TO LIVE WITH HER EXILED LOVER.

VOLUME II
CHAPTER VII

ONE NIGHT, IN THE WOOD, I FOUND SOME BOOKS IN A LEATHER CASE.

MY CREATOR HAD ABANDONED ME - AND IN THE BITTERNESS OF MY HEART, I CURSED HIM.

I WAITED FOR THE RIGHT MOMENT TO INTRODUCE MYSELF TO THE COTTAGERS.

MONTHS PASSED; THEN, ONE DAY, WHEN THE OLD MAN WAS LEFT ALONE, I APPROACHED THE DOOR OF THE COTTAGE...

KNOCK KNOCK

WHO'S THERE? COME IN.

PARDON ME - I'M A TRAVELLER IN NEED OF REST.

COME IN, BUT AS I'M BLIND, I CAN'T OFFER YOU ANY FOOD.

ALL I WANT IS WARMTH AND REST.

CRACK!

HE THREW ME TO THE GROUND. I COULD HAVE TORN HIM APART - BUT MY HEART SANK WITH SADNESS, AND I STOPPED MYSELF.

OVERCOME BY PAIN, I LEFT THE COTTAGE AND ESCAPED UNSEEN TO MY HOVEL.

VOLUME II
CHAPTER VIII

THE FAMILY ABANDONED THE COTTAGE.

IN MY RAGE, I LIT THE DRY BRANCH OF A TREE, AND THE COTTAGE WAS SOON ON FIRE.

AND NOW, WHERE SHOULD I GO?

I LEARNT FROM YOUR PAPERS THAT YOU WERE MY CREATOR, AND THAT YOU WERE FROM GENEVA...

...SO THAT'S WHERE I HEADED.

MY TRAVELS WERE LONG. I RESTED DURING THE DAY AND TRAVELLED AT NIGHT WHEN I WAS SURE I WOULDN'T BE SEEN.

ONE MORNING, AS I WALKED THROUGH A DEEP WOOD, I DECIDED TO CONTINUE AFTER SUNRISE. IT WAS A BEAUTIFUL SPRING DAY.

HEARING VOICES, I HID. A YOUNG GIRL RAN ALONG THE SIDE OF THE RIVER.

SHE SLIPPED AND FELL INTO THE RAPID STREAM!

AFTER SOME WEEKS, MY WOUND HEALED; I CONTINUED MY JOURNEY, AND IN TWO MONTHS, I APPROACHED GENEVA.

I FELL ASLEEP...

...ONLY TO BE DISTURBED BY A CHILD APPROACHING.

I THOUGHT THAT HE WAS STILL TOO YOUNG AND INNOCENT TO FIND ME HORRIBLE.

AAAHHH!

IF I COULD SEIZE HIM, AND TEACH HIM TO BE MY FRIEND, THEN I WOULD NO LONGER BE ALONE.

FRANKENSTEIN!

YOU BELONG TO MY ENEMY!

THEN YOU WILL BE MY FIRST VICTIM!

THE CHILD STRUGGLED. I GRASPED HIS THROAT TO SILENCE HIM...

...AND IN A MOMENT HE WAS DEAD.

I TOO CAN CREATE SORROW! THIS DEATH SHALL TORMENT AND DESTROY MY ENEMY!

AROUND HIS NECK, I SAW A PICTURE OF A BEAUTIFUL WOMAN.

I WOULD NEVER KNOW THE DELIGHTS SUCH BEAUTY COULD BRING.

FOR DAYS I STAYED **CLOSE** TO THE **SCENE** OF THE MURDER. I WANDERED TO THESE MOUNTAINS - WITH AN **OBSESSION** THAT ONLY YOU CAN SATISFY.

YOU MUST NOW **PROMISE** TO DO AS I ASK. I AM **ALONE** AND **MISERABLE.** MAN HATES ME --

-- SO YOU MUST CREATE A **WOMAN** WHO IS **JUST LIKE ME;** SHE WILL NOT **DENY** HERSELF TO ME.

VOLUME II
CHAPTER IX

ONLY YOU CAN DO THIS - YOU **MUST NOT** REFUSE.

**NO!**

YOU CAN **TORTURE ME,** BUT I'LL **NEVER** DO **THAT!**

I AM ONLY **EVIL** BECAUSE I AM **MISERABLE.**

LET ME BE **GRATEFUL** TO YOU FOR **JUST** THIS **ONE THING!**

DO NOT **DENY ME** THIS!

ALTHOUGH I *SHUDDERED* AT THE *THOUGHT*, HIS *ARGUMENT* MADE *SENSE*.

HOW CAN YOU *LIVE* AWAY FROM *HUMAN KIND*?

I GIVE YOU MY WORD.

IF YOU AGREE TO THIS, NEITHER *YOU*, NOR *ANY* OTHER HUMAN SHALL EVER SEE US AGAIN.

WE SHALL LIVE *PEACEFULLY*.

HOW CAN I *TRUST* YOU?

YOU WILL *RETURN*, AND YOUR *EVIL PASSIONS* WILL BE *RENEWED*.

THE *LOVE* OF ANOTHER WILL REMOVE THE REASON FOR MY CRIMES.

I'LL *DO IT*, AS LONG AS YOU *PROMISE* TO *LEAVE EUROPE FOREVER* AND *NEVER* VISIT *ANY AREA INHABITED* BY *MAN*.

I PROMISE –
IF YOU GRANT
MY PRAYER, YOU
SHALL **NEVER**
SEE ME
AGAIN!

GO HOME,
AND MAKE A **START.**
I SHALL WATCH YOUR
**PROGRESS** – AND WHEN
YOU ARE **READY,** I
SHALL **APPEAR!**

*I SAW HIM **DESCEND** THE **MOUNTAIN**
WITH **GREAT SPEED** AND **DISAPPEAR.***

*WITH A **HEAVY HEART,**
I **DESCENDED**
TOWARDS THE **VALLEY.***

*I RETURNED **HOME** TO
MY **FAMILY** IN **GENEVA.**

I COULD HARDLY **SPEAK;**
YET I **LOVED** THEM WITH
ALL MY **HEART.** TO **SAVE**
THEM, I **DEDICATED**
MYSELF TO THIS **MOST
HORRIBLE TASK.***

IN **THAT** CASE, WE SHALL **ALL** BE HAPPY. **TELL** ME, THEN - WOULD YOU **OBJECT** TO AN **IMMEDIATE** MARRIAGE?

*I WAS **UNABLE** TO ANSWER MY **FATHER**.*

*I COULDN'T **THINK** ABOUT MARRYING **ELIZABETH** UNTIL I HAD **COMPLETED** THE TASK FOR THE **MONSTER**.*

*THE **MONSTER** MUST DEPART WITH HIS **MATE** BEFORE I COULD **ENJOY** MY FUTURE LIFE IN **PEACE**.*

*I NEEDED TO TRAVEL TO **ENGLAND** TO GAIN **NEW** INFORMATION FOR MY **TASK**. IT WAS **ALSO** IMPORTANT FOR ME TO BE **AWAY** FROM ALL I **LOVED**.*

*THESE MATTERS DECIDED THE **ANSWER** I GAVE TO MY **FATHER**.*

85

I MADE MY **FATHER AGREE** TO THE **TRIP**.

HE **INSISTED** THAT I TAKE **HENRY CLERVAL** WITH ME.

ALTHOUGH I NEEDED TO BE **ALONE** FOR MY **WORK**, CLERVAL'S **COMPANY** WOULD **SAVE ME** FROM **HOURS** OF **LONELY, MADDENING THOUGHT**.

HAVING HIM THERE MIGHT EVEN **STOP** THE **MONSTER** FROM WANTING TO **VISIT** ME.

I WAS TO **MARRY ELIZABETH** WHEN I **RETURNED** - A **PEACEFUL** LIFE WITH MY **BELOVED** WAS THE **ONE REWARD** FOR MY **HORRID TASK**.

BUT WHAT IF HE DIDN'T **FOLLOW** ME? HE COULD **ATTACK** MY **FAMILY** WHILE I WAS **AWAY** IN **ENGLAND**.

**NO** - HE **SAID** THAT HE WOULD **FOLLOW** ME **WHEREVER** I WENT. MY **FAMILY** AND **FRIENDS** WERE **SAFE**.

I ONLY VISITED THESE PEOPLE FOR INFORMATION.

UNLIKE CLERVAL, I COULDN'T BRING MYSELF TO ENJOY THEIR COMPANY.

CLERVAL WAS JUST AS I USED TO BE: ANXIOUS, INQUISITIVE, AND KEEN TO ACCOMPLISH SOMETHING.

HE WANTED TO VISIT INDIA SO THAT HE COULD LEARN ABOUT TRADE THERE.

HE WAS ALWAYS BUSY; I OFTEN TOLD HIM I HAD TO GO SOMEWHERE ELSE - JUST SO THAT I COULD BE ALONE.

I NOW ALSO BEGAN TO COLLECT THE MATERIALS THAT I NEEDED...

...FOR MY NEW CREATION.

WE RECEIVED AN **INVITATION** TO VISIT AN OLD **FRIEND** IN **SCOTLAND.** **CLERVAL** EAGERLY **ACCEPTED;** ALTHOUGH I **HATED** THE IDEA OF **MEETING** PEOPLE, I **LONGED** TO SEE **MOUNTAINS** AGAIN.

ON THE **WAY** WE VISITED **WINDSOR, OXFORD, MATLOCK,** AND THE **CUMBERLAND LAKES.**

I TOOK MY **INSTRUMENTS** AND **MATERIALS,** SO THAT I COULD **FINISH** MY WORK IN THE **SCOTTISH HIGHLANDS.**

CLERVAL **LOVED** EDINBURGH - BUT I WAS **EAGER** TO GET TO THE **END** OF MY **JOURNEY.**

SOMETIMES I FELT THAT THE **MONSTER** MIGHT **MURDER** MY **FRIEND,** SO THAT HE MIGHT **REFOCUS** MY **EFFORTS.**

IT WAS AS IF I HAD **COMMITTED** SOME **CRIME.** I WAS **GUILTLESS,** BUT I HAD PLACED A **HORRIBLE CURSE** UPON MY OWN HEAD - AS REAL AS ANY **CRIME.**

I FOUND A **REMOTE SPOT** IN THE **NORTHERN HIGHLANDS** WHERE I COULD **FINISH** MY WORK **ALONE.**

ONLY **FIVE PEOPLE** LIVED THERE, ALONG WITH A FEW **COWS,** ON THE **BARREN LAND.** IT WAS **PERFECT!**

WHEN I **FIRST ARRIVED,** I **WORKED** BY **DAY,** AND SPENT THE **EVENINGS** WALKING ON THE **STONY BEACH.**

BUT AS THE DAYS PASSED, I BEGAN TO HATE MY WORK. SOMETIMES, I COULD NOT BRING MYSELF TO ENTER MY LABORATORY...

...AND AT OTHER TIMES, I WORKED DAY AND NIGHT IN A KIND OF FEVER. EVERY MOMENT, I FEARED TO MEET THE MONSTER.

MY FIRST EXPERIMENT HAD BEEN FUELLED BY EXCITEMENT...

...BUT NOW MY HEART WAS SICKENED AT THE WORK OF MY HANDS.

VOLUME III
CHAPTER III

I SUDDENLY THOUGHT ABOUT WHAT I WAS ACTUALLY DOING.

THREE YEARS AGO I HAD CREATED A MONSTER; AND HE HAD DESTROYED LIFE.

I WAS NOW ABOUT TO CREATE YET ANOTHER MONSTER; AND WHO COULD TELL WHAT IT MIGHT DO?

THE MONSTER *HAD* FOLLOWED ME HERE, AND *NOW* HE CAME TO *CLAIM* HIS *PRIZE.*

HE *LOOKED EVIL...*

...AND THE *THOUGHT* OF *CREATING ANOTHER LIKE HIM* DROVE ME TO *MADNESS.*

AAAARRRGGGHHH!

THUNK!

SQUELCH!

THUDD!

THE **MONSTER** WATCHED IN **HORROR** AS I **DESTROYED** THE **ONLY** **CREATURE** THAT COULD BRING HIM **FUTURE HAPPINESS.**

WITH A *HOWL* OF *DEVILISH DESPAIR*, HE *DISAPPEARED*.

I *VOWED* NEVER TO *RESUME* MY *LABOURS*.

ALONE FOR *HOURS*, THE *SILENCE* WAS *BROKEN* BY THE *SOUND* OF *OARS...*

YOU HAVE *DESTROYED* YOUR *WORK!* DO YOU INTEND TO *BREAK* YOUR *PROMISE* TO ME?

*BEGONE!*

I WILL *NEVER* CREATE ANYTHING LIKE YOU AGAIN!

SLAVE, I AM *MORE POWERFUL* THAN YOU.

YOU ARE MY *CREATOR*, BUT I AM YOUR *MASTER* – *OBEY!*

BEFORE YOU **KILL ME**, BE **SURE** OF YOUR **OWN SAFETY!**

HE **DISAPPEARED** IN HIS **BOAT**, AND **ALL** WAS **SILENT AGAIN**.

I THOUGHT **AGAIN** OF HIS **WORDS**...

"I SHALL BE **WITH YOU** ON YOUR **WEDDING NIGHT**."

**THAT**, THEN, WAS THE **DATE** SET FOR MY **DESTINY. TEARS**, THE **FIRST** I'D **CRIED** FOR **MANY MONTHS**, STREAMED FROM MY **EYES** WHEN I THOUGHT OF **ELIZABETH** FINDING HER **LOVER SNATCHED** FROM HER.

I DECIDED **NOT TO GIVE** IN WITHOUT A **FIGHT**.

THE NEXT **DAY**, I RECEIVED A **LETTER** FROM **CLERVAL** ASKING ME TO **JOIN HIM**. THE **LETTER** BROUGHT ME **BACK** TO **REALITY**.

I FOUND THE **COURAGE** TO ENTER MY **LABORATORY**, TO PACK UP MY **INSTRUMENTS** AND THE **REMAINS** OF THE **HALF-FINISHED CREATURE**.

IN THE **EARLY MORNING**, I SAILED **OUT** AND **CAST** THEM INTO THE **SEA**.

THE **QUIET** OF THE **BOAT** ON THE **WAVES** LULLED ME INTO A **PEACEFUL SLEEP**...

WHEN I **AWOKE**, THE **SUN** WAS HIGH - BUT THE **WIND** WAS EVEN **HIGHER:** THREATENING THE **SAFETY** OF MY **LITTLE BOAT.**

I TRIED TO CHANGE MY **COURSE...**

...BUT MY **BOAT** STARTED TO **FILL** WITH **WATER.** MY **ONLY** HOPE WAS TO GO IN THE **DIRECTION** OF THE WIND. I HAD NO **COMPASS**, AND WAS **UTTERLY LOST.**

I THOUGHT THE **SEA** WAS GOING TO BE MY **GRAVE.**

**MONSTER!** YOU'VE **FINALLY GOT** WHAT YOU **WANTED!**

**HOURS** PASSED...

...UNTIL THE **WIND** CHANGED TO A **BREEZE.** I WAS SO **TIRED,** THAT I FELT **SICK...** ...WHEN **SUDDENLY,** I SAW **LAND.**

**TEARS** GUSHED FROM MY **EYES** WHEN I **KNEW** I WAS **FINALLY SAFE.**

VOLUME III
CHAPTER IV

THE *JUDGE* WAS A *KINDLY MAN* - HOWEVER, HE LOOKED *HARSHLY* TOWARDS *ME.*

WHO APPEARS AS A *WITNESS?*

ME, SIR.

I HAD BEEN OUT *FISHING* WITH MY *BROTHER-IN-LAW,* DANIEL *NUGENT.*

ON THE *SANDS,* I *STUMBLED* ON THE BODY OF THE *DEAD* MAN. HIS *CLOTHES* WERE *DRY,* SO HE HADN'T *DROWNED.* IT *LOOKED* LIKE HE'D BEEN *STRANGLED* --

-- BECAUSE THERE WERE *BLACK FINGER MARKS* ON HIS *NECK.*

I REMEMBERED THE *MURDER* OF MY *BROTHER,* AND I *TREMBLED.*

MR. KIRWIN *SAW* HOW THIS *INFORMATION AFFECTED* ME: IT MADE ME APPEAR *GUILTY* OF THE CRIME.

DANIEL NUGENT, SIR.

JUST BEFORE WE FOUND THE *BODY,* I SAW A *MAN* JUST OFF THE *SHORE* IN A SMALL *BOAT* -

*JUST* LIKE THE ONE THAT *THIS MAN* LANDED IN.

102

A **WOMAN** ALSO SAW A **BOAT** WITH A **MAN** IN IT **LEAVE** THE **SHORE** WHERE THE **CORPSE** WAS FOUND.

THEY ALL **AGREED** THAT WITH THE **STRONG WIND**, I'D BEEN **DRIVEN BACK** TO THE **SHORE** WHERE I'D **LEFT** THE **BODY**.

**SHOW** HIM THE **BODY** — I WANT TO **SEE** HOW HE **REACTS**.

I WAS **RELAXED**...

...BECAUSE I **KNEW** THAT THE **PEOPLE** ON THE **ISLAND** I HAD **LEFT** COULD **PROVE** MY **INNOCENCE**.

**NO!!** MY **DEAREST HENRY!!** NOT **YOU** TOO!!!

**OTHER** VICTIMS **AWAIT** THEIR **DESTINY**...

...BUT **YOU**, **CLERVAL**, MY **FRIEND**...

THEY HAD TO **CARRY ME OUT** OF THE **ROOM**.

FRIGHTFUL RAVINGS, IN A FITFUL FEVER FOLLOWED FOR *TWO MONTHS*.

I CALLED *MYSELF* THE *MURDERER* OF *WILLIAM, JUSTINE* AND OF *CLERVAL*.

FORTUNATELY, ONLY *MR. KIRWIN* UNDERSTOOD MY *NATIVE LANGUAGE* - BUT MY CRIES *FRIGHTENED* THE PEOPLE *AROUND* ME.

WHY DID I NOT *DIE?* I WAS MORE *MISERABLE* THAN *ANY* MAN HAD BEEN *BEFORE.*

BUT I WAS *DOOMED* TO *LIVE.* AFTER TWO MONTHS, I *AWOKE* IN *PRISON.*

ARE YOU *BETTER* NOW, SIR?

I *BELIEVE* I AM;

BUT I'M *SORRY* THAT I'M *STILL* ALIVE TO FEEL THIS *MISERY* AND *HORROR.*

IT WOULD BE **BETTER** IF YOU **WERE** DEAD, BUT THAT'S NOT FOR **ME** TO SAY.

I WAS **SENT HERE** TO LOOK **AFTER YOU** - AND I'M JUST DOING MY **DUTY.**

I SOON **LEARNED** THAT MR. **KIRWIN** HAD BEEN **KIND** TO ME BY PROVIDING A **DOCTOR** AND A **NURSE.**

HE **VISITED ME** AS SOON AS I HAD **RECOVERED.**

I'M **WORRIED** THAT THIS PLACE IS **ADDING** TO YOUR **MISERY.**

AS **SOON** AS YOU WERE TAKEN **ILL,** I LOOKED THROUGH THE **PAPERS** THAT YOU WERE CARRYING AND FOUND A **LETTER** FROM YOUR **FATHER** IN GENEVA.

OH **NO!!**

**WHO** HAS BEEN **KILLED NOW?!?**

YOUR **FAMILY** IS PERFECTLY **WELL...**

I HAD TO **TRAVEL** NEARLY A **HUNDRED MILES** TO APPEAR IN THE **COUNTY COURT.** **MR. KIRWIN** ARRANGED MY **DEFENCE.**

THE **GRAND JURY** FOUND ME **INNOCENT.**

SOON **AFTERWARDS,** I WAS **RELEASED** FROM **PRISON** - **FREE** TO **BREATHE** THE **FRESH AIR,** AND ABLE TO **RETURN** TO **GENEVA.**

BUT FOR **ME, WHEREVER** I WENT WAS **HATEFUL.** MY LIFE HAD BEEN **POISONED FOREVER.**

I THOUGHT ABOUT **ENDING** MY **LIFE** - YET **ONE DUTY** REMAINED: I HAD TO **LOOK AFTER** THOSE PEOPLE I SO **FONDLY LOVED...** ...AND I HAD TO **LIE IN WAIT** FOR THE **MURDERER.**

## VOLUME III
## CHAPTER V

WHEN WE REACHED *PARIS*, I RECEIVED A *LETTER* FROM *ELIZABETH*:

*...TELL ME*, DEAREST *VICTOR* - DO YOU *LOVE ANOTHER?*

I *CONFESS* MY *LOVE* TO YOU, BUT IT IS *YOUR HAPPINESS* THAT I DESIRE, AS *WELL* AS MY *OWN*.

- ELIZABETH

I *REMEMBERED* THE *THREAT* OF THE *FIEND* - "I SHALL BE WITH YOU ON YOUR *WEDDING NIGHT*."

ON *THAT NIGHT* HE HAD DECIDED TO *KILL ME*. OH, SWEET *ELIZABETH* - I WOULD *DIE* TO MAKE HER *HAPPY*.

MY *BELOVED ELIZABETH*, I *FEAR* THAT LITTLE *HAPPINESS* REMAINS FOR US ON *EARTH*; YET ALL MY *FUTURE* HAPPINESS IS CENTRED ON *YOU*.

I HAVE *ONE*, *DREADFUL SECRET* WHICH WILL *FILL YOU* WITH *HORROR* - AND I WILL *CONFESS* THIS TO YOU THE *DAY AFTER* OUR *MARRIAGE*. UNTIL *THEN*, YOU MUST *NOT MENTION* IT.

- VICTOR

WE *RETURNED* TO *GENEVA*, WHERE ELIZABETH *WELCOMED* ME WITH *WARM AFFECTION*.

MY **FATHER** HAD ARRANGED FOR **ELIZABETH** TO INHERIT A SMALL **VILLA** ON THE SHORES OF **LAKE COMO**, WHICH BELONGED TO HER **FAMILY**. WE PLANNED TO SPEND OUR **FIRST DAYS** THERE.

WE **COMMENCED** OUR JOURNEY BY **WATER**, HEADING TOWARDS **EVIAN**, WHERE WE WOULD **STAY** THE **NIGHT**.

YOU ARE **SORROWFUL**, MY **LOVE**.

IF YOU **KNEW** HOW I HAVE **SUFFERED**, YOU WOULD TRY TO LET ME **ENJOY** TODAY.

BE **HAPPY**, **VICTOR**.

I **FEEL** THAT **SOMETHING BAD** MAY HAPPEN, BUT I **WON'T LISTEN** TO **THOSE** VOICES.

WHAT A **DIVINE DAY**!

THOSE WERE THE **LAST MOMENTS** OF MY **LIFE** WHEN I **ENJOYED** THE **FEELING** OF **HAPPINESS**.

AS WE REACHED THE **SHORE**, I FELT THE **FEAR** THAT WAS TO **CLING** TO ME **FOREVER**.

VOLUME III
CHAPTER VI

WE TOOK A *SHORT WALK* ALONG THE *SHORE.*

A *VIOLENT STORM* CAME - *WATCHFUL* AND *ANXIOUS,* I *REACHED* FOR MY *PISTOL.*

WHAT *IS IT,* VICTOR?

IT'LL BE *ALL RIGHT,* MY *LOVE.*

IT'S *JUST A BAD STORM.*

PLEASE GO TO *BED,* ELIZABETH - I WILL *JOIN* YOU *LATER.*

VICTOR...

I SEARCHED EVERYWHERE FOR THE MONSTER...

...BUT I DISCOVERED NO TRACE OF HIM.

AAAAHH!!!

SHRIEK!!

I REALISED WHAT WAS HAPPENING!

ELIZABETH!!!

I FELL, SENSELESS, TO THE GROUND.

WHEN I *RECOVERED,* I RUSHED *TOWARDS* HER AND *HELD* HER IN MY *ARMS.*

LIKE HIS *OTHER VICTIMS,* THE *MONSTER* HAD *STRANGLED* MY *BELOVED ELIZABETH!*

I LOOKED *UP* AT THE *WINDOW...*

...TO SEE THE *MONSTER SMIRKING* AND *POINTING* TOWARDS THE *DEAD BODY* OF MY *WIFE.*

B-LAM

**KA-BLAM!**

HE *GOT AWAY,* AND *PLUNGED* INTO THE *LAKE.*

THE *SOUND* OF THE *GUNFIRE* ATTRACTED A *CROWD,* WHO *HELPED* ME TO *LOOK* FOR THE *FIEND.* AFTER *SEVERAL HOURS,* WE *GAVE UP* THE SEARCH.

I WAS IN *SHOCK.*

THE *DEATHS* OF *WILLIAM, JUSTINE, CLERVAL,* AND NOW MY *WIFE...*

...MY *FATHER* AND *ERNEST* MIGHT BE *NEXT!*

I DECIDED TO *RETURN IMMEDIATELY* TO GENEVA.

MY FATHER AND ERNEST WERE SAFE, BUT THE NEWS OF ELIZABETH'S DEATH WAS HARD FOR MY FATHER TO BEAR.

CURSED BE THE FIEND THAT BROUGHT MISERY ON HIS GREY HAIRS.

IT WAS ALL TOO MUCH FOR HIM, AND IN A FEW DAYS HE DIED IN MY ARMS.

WHAT BECAME OF ME THEN? I DON'T KNOW...

...I LOST MY SENSES, AND WAS CHAINED UP IN A DARK, SOLITARY CELL. THEY CALLED ME MAD.

WHEN I WAS **WELL ENOUGH** TO BE **RELEASED**, I VISITED A **CRIMINAL JUDGE** TO TELL HIM MY **STORY**.

SIR, I **KNOW** THE **MURDERER**,

AND I **WANT YOU** TO INSTRUCT THE **AUTHORITIES** TO FIND HIM.

SIR, I'LL DO **ALL** THAT I **CAN**.

**THANK YOU.**

MY **TALE** MAY BE VERY **STRANGE**, BUT I CAN **ASSURE YOU**, IT IS **ALL TRUE**...

I TOLD MY **STORY**, GIVING **DATES** FOR **ACCURACY**.

IT IS YOUR **DUTY**, NOW, TO **SEIZE** AND **PUNISH** THIS VILLAIN.

I DON'T THINK WE'D **EVER** BE ABLE TO **CATCH** THIS **CREATURE**.

**BESIDES** - WHO **KNOWS** WHERE HE MAY BE **LIVING** NOW.

YOU **REFUSE** TO **HELP** ME!

THEN I'LL **DO IT MYSELF** - I WON'T **REST** UNTIL HE IS **DESTROYED**!!

I FOLLOWED *CLUES* AROUND THE *WORLD*, AND *STILL* HE *EVADED* ME.

MY LIFE WAS *HATEFUL* TO *ME*, AS I *FOLLOWED* HIS *TAUNTING MESSAGES*. THEN, WITH A *SLEDGE* AND *DOGS*, I *FINALLY* STARTED TO *GAIN* ON HIM...

...AND HAD *ALMOST REACHED* HIM, WHEN THE *ICE SPLIT* AND *CRACKED*.

I *THOUGHT* I WAS ABOUT TO *SINK*, WHEN I *SAW* YOUR *SHIP APPROACHING*.

I *DREAD DEATH* - FOR MY *TASK* IS *UNFINISHED*; BUT IF I *DIE*, WALTON, *SWEAR* TO ME THAT YOU WILL *FIND* AND *KILL* HIM.

117

LETTER - SEPTEMBER 7TH.

THE **MATTER** IS **SETTLED**. IF WE ARE **FREED** FROM THE **ICE**, I HAVE **AGREED** TO **RETURN HOME**.

September 12th.

I am returning to England.
I have lost my hopes of glory - and I have lost my friend.

Three days ago, the ice began to move. By this time, my unfortunate guest was entirely confined to his bed.

THEY **SHOUT** BECAUSE THEY WILL **SOON** BE **HEADING BACK HOME**.

HURRAH!

YEAH!

HOORAY!

ARE YOU **REALLY** GOING HOME?

ALAS **YES**; I CANNOT **LEAD** THEM INTO **FURTHER DANGER**, AND I **MUST RETURN**.

I DO NOT LOOK FOR SYMPATHY. I AM CONTENT TO SUFFER ALONE.

ONCE I HOPED FOR HUMAN FRIENDSHIP, BUT NOW CRIME HAS PUT ME BENEATH THE LOWEST CREATURE.

NO GUILT OR MISERY CAN BE FOUND THAT COMPARES TO MINE.

WHEN I REMEMBER ALL THAT I HAVE DONE, I CANNOT BELIEVE THAT I AM THE SAME CREATURE THAT ONCE WANTED ONLY GOODNESS.

THE FALLEN ANGEL HAS BECOME A TERRIBLE, SOLITARY, DEVIL.

SOON I SHALL DIE - AND THESE *BURNING* MISERIES WILL *END*. I SHALL REJOICE IN THE AGONY OF THE *TORTURING FLAMES*!

GRAAARRRRGGGHHH!!!

THE *LIGHT* OF THE FIRE WILL *FADE AWAY*, AND MY ASHES SHALL BE *SCATTERED* BY THE WINDS...

...AND MY SPIRIT WILL *SLEEP* IN PEACE.

FAREWELL! YOU SHALL BE THE LAST HUMAN I SHALL SEE.

FAREWELL, FRANKENSTEIN! AS MISERABLE AS YOU WERE --

-- MY AGONY WAS STILL GREATER THAN YOURS!

THUDD!!!

HE WAS SOON *FAR AWAY* - LOST IN THE *DARKNESS AND DISTANCE.*

# Frankenstein

## End

# Mary Shelley

## 1797-1851

"It is not singular that, as the daughter of two persons of distinguished literary celebrity, I should very early in life have thought of writing."

Mary Shelley was born Mary Wollstonecraft Godwin in Somers Town, London in August 1797. Her father, William Godwin, was a famous philosopher, novelist and journalist. Her mother was Mary Wollstonecraft, who was a feminist philosopher, educator, and writer, well known for her work, *A Vindication of the Rights of Woman* (1792). In it, she argued that women are not naturally inferior to men, but appear that way due to a lack of education (education did not become compulsory in England until the Education Act of 1870). She suggested that both men and women should be treated equally, and as rational beings in a society that operated upon reason and logic.

Despite William and Mary's revolutionary attitudes to the social order of the time, and the fact that Mary already had a daughter, Fanny Imlay, from a previous relationship, they married in March 1797 to ensure the legitimacy of their coming child.

Sadly, Mary Wollstonecraft died of puerperal fever (sometimes called "childbed fever") a few days after giving birth, leaving William Godwin alone to bring up baby Mary and her older half-sister Fanny. He believed himself **"totally unfitted to educate them"**, and felt that a substitute mother should be found. He didn't look far! William Godwin married his next-door neighbour, Mary Jane Vial (better known as Mary Jane Clairmont) on 21st December 1801. Mary Jane brought two children of her own into the marriage: Charles and Jane (who later called herself Claire). Then, in 1803, Mary Jane gave birth to William Godwin Junior - bringing the total to five children living under the same roof.

Mary Wollstonecraft Godwin did not have a "formal" education, but was taught to read and write at home. Her father encouraged her to write from an early age. She was given freedom to access his extensive library, and allowed to listen to the political, philosophical, scientific and literary discussions that he conducted with his friends —William Wordsworth and Samuel Taylor Coleridge were among the many distinguished visitors to the house at this time.

William and Jane Godwin started a publishing company in 1805 (M. Godwin and Co.) and opened a shop selling children's books. The couple also wrote children's books themselves, often under the name of Edward Baldwin.

In 1810, they published what was possibly Mary's first work: *Mounseer*

*Nongtongpaw; or the Discoveries of John Bull on a Trip to Paris,* a verse poem. It is hard to say whether this was in fact Mary's first work, as all of her early papers were lost, and nothing of her surviving writing can be dated prior to 1814 with any certainty.

In 1812, possibly due to growing conflict with her stepmother, Mary went to live for several months in Dundee with the family of William Baxter, who was a friend of her father's.

Around the same time, the famous poet Percy Bysshe Shelley (a devoted follower, friend and sponsor of Mary's father) began spending a great deal of time in the Godwin home. Percy, along with his young wife Harriet and sister-in-law Eliza, would regularly dine there; and Mary would have met Percy on her return visits to London. By then, aged nineteen, Shelley had already been expelled from Oxford University and his family would only talk to him through lawyers.

Percy and Mary began to meet outside of her home, often at the grave of Mary's mother in St. Pancras Churchyard, where Mary used to sit and read her mother's works. Their relationship developed quickly - much to the horror of Mary's father, who forbade the lovers to meet.

Disregarding the views of her father and of society as a whole, on 18th July 1814, when Mary was only sixteen years old, the lovers ran away to France, taking Jane Clairmont (Mary's stepsister, who later called herself Claire) with them. Mary also took a box containing her writings and letters; and unfortunately, this precious box was lost during the journey.

After only two months, the travellers returned to London. They were penniless, and Shelley was forced to hide from people he owed money to. Mary's father still strongly disapproved of the relationship and would not even meet with his daughter or her lover. Mary, unmarried and barely seventeen, was now pregnant. To make matters worse, Percy Shelley's wife, Harriet, was also pregnant. Harriet gave birth to a son in 1814 and sued her husband for custody of their children and for financial support - leaving Percy in terrible financial difficulty.

From her sparse journal entries of this time, it would appear that the young couple still enjoyed a reasonable standard of living, and had a close circle of friends — which was surprising as their behaviour would have been considered scandalous by the "respectable" society of the day.

Percy Shelley's grandfather, Sir Bysshe Shelley, died in January 1815. This left Percy as "heir apparent" to the title and to the family estate on the death of his father. It also greatly improved the Shelleys' financial situation; and by June 1815, Percy was in receipt of an annual allowance of £1,000 — a huge amount of money at a time when the average annual wage for a weaver was only £16 (six shillings per-week).

However, the relationship between Mary and Percy was sadly to be put under further strain. Their first daughter was born two months premature, and died within a few days. This was to have a lasting effect on Mary, as she wrote in her journal on 19th March 1815:

> "Dream that my little baby came to life again -- that it had only been cold & that we rubbed it by the fire & it lived -- I awake & find no baby -- I think about the little thing all day -- not in good spirits -- Shelley is very unwell."

Almost immediately, Mary became pregnant again; and a second, healthy child, William, was born a year later. During this time, Shelley's health was deteriorating (possibly through a weak heart) and the continuing but not always welcome presence of Mary's

stepsister - now known as Claire - can only have added further pressure to the couple's relationship.

The following year of 1816 was no less eventful. Claire had become pregnant by the poet Lord George Byron. She needed to establish with Byron that the child was indeed his, and so persuaded Percy and Mary to accompany her to Switzerland to meet him at Lake Geneva. By June, they had settled near Cologny - and it was here that Mary began to write *Frankenstein*; she was still only eighteen. In her original preface to the book, she wrote:

> "I passed the summer of 1816 in the environs of Geneva. The season was cold and rainy, and in the evenings we crowded around a blazing wood fire, and occasionally amused ourselves with some German stories of ghosts, which happened to fall into our hands. These tales excited in us a playful desire of imitation. Two other friends (a tale from the pen of one of whom would be far more acceptable to the public than any thing I can ever hope to produce) and myself agreed to write each a story founded on some supernatural occurrence."

They returned to London in September 1816. In October, Mary's older half-sister Fanny committed suicide through a laudanum overdose. In November, Percy Shelley's pregnant wife Harriet went missing, and was eventually found drowned in the River Serpentine. She was just twenty-one years old - and her death greatly added to the scandal that already dogged the couple. Amidst all of this drama, Mary Wollstonecraft married Percy Shelley on 30th December 1816 at St Mildred's Church in London.

*Frankenstein* was eventually completed in May 1817, but wasn't published until 1818 — and even then, Mary wasn't named as the author (*Frankenstein* wasn't published in her name until 1831).

In September 1817, Mary gave birth to her third child, Clara Everina. Percy owed money once again, and the family, along with Claire and her young child, moved across Europe towards the warmer climes of Italy.

Tragically, Clara Everina died in Venice in 1818; and in the following year, their son William died of Malaria in Rome. These losses had a profound effect on Mary, who sank into a deep depression. Percy wrote in his notebook:

> "My dearest Mary, wherefore hast thou gone,
> And left me in this dreary world alone?
> Thy form is here indeed—a lovely one—
> But thou art fled, gone down a dreary road
> That leads to Sorrow's most obscure abode.
> For thine own sake I cannot follow thee
> Do thou return for mine."

The Shelleys moved to Florence in October 1819, where their son Percy Florence was born the following month. His birth lifted Mary's spirits and brought the couple closer together again.

In May 1822, they moved on to La Spezia, where Mary miscarried on 16th June during her fifth pregnancy. Percy insisted that she should sit in a bath of ice until the doctor arrived — and that advice saved her life.

Percy Shelley was not a strong swimmer, and some say that he couldn't swim at all; yet despite that, and even though he had once nearly drowned in a boating accident, he and several friends decided to spend the summer of 1822 sailing on the Bay of Lerici. On 18th July, the drowned bodies of Percy, his friend Edward Williams and a young sailor by

the name of Charles Vivian were washed ashore. In keeping with the quarantine regulations of the time, Percy Shelley's body was cremated on the beach near Viareggio. His heart was snatched from the funeral pyre by Edward Trelawny - adventurer, author and friend of the poets — who had designed the boat that sank.

In 1823, Shelley's ashes were interred in a burial plot in the Cimitero Acattolico in Rome, under an ancient pyramid in the city walls. The Latin inscription reads, "Cor Cordium", which translates to "Heart of Hearts". It also bears a few lines from Shakespeare's *The Tempest*:

> "Nothing of him that doth fade
> But doth suffer a sea change
> into something rich & strange"

Back in England, *The Courier* (a leading newspaper of the time) published a notice of the death of Shelley:-

> "Shelley, the writer of some infidel poetry has been drowned; now he knows whether there is a God or no."

Mary and her only surviving child, Percy Florence, left Italy in the summer of 1823 and returned to England.

Percy Shelley's allowance ended when he died. His father, Sir Timothy Shelley, provided Mary and his grandson with only a very small sum of money — and even that was on the condition that she did not publish any of his son's remaining manuscripts, and that she did not write under her married name.

It is to satisfy this last condition that all of her publications avoid the use of an author's name, and instead say, "By the Author of *Frankenstein*."

In 1824 she wrote in her journal:

> "At the age of twenty six I am in the condition of an aged person--all my old friends are gone ... & my heart fails when I think by how few ties I hold to the world...."

She did not remarry; in fact she turned down more than one proposal, saying that after being married to one genius, she could only marry another. She concentrated on earning money from her writing, while looking after her father, William, until his death in 1836. Percy Florence followed in his father's footsteps, going to public school and on to university. He inherited his grandfather's baronetcy in 1844, becoming Sir Percy Florence Shelley, 3rd Baronet.

Although Mary continued to write, none of her later works are as well known or as powerful as her first novel, *Frankenstein* (she died before completing the biography of her husband). From 1839 onwards, she suffered from several illnesses, including headaches and bouts of paralysis, which at times prevented her from writing; and she was blighted by ill health in her final years. In 1848, Percy Florence married Jane Gibson St John. Mary shared her time between living with them at their country home in Sussex, and at her own home in Chester Square, London.

Mary Wollstonecraft Shelley died on 1st February 1851 aged fifty-three. The cause of death is recorded as "Disease of the brain – supposed tumour in left hemisphere of long standing". She is buried next to her parents at St. Peter's Church in Bournemouth.

After her death, Mary's box desk was opened. In it were locks of her dead children's hair, a notebook she had shared with Percy Bysshe Shelley, and a copy of his poem, *Adonaïs*, with one page folded around a silk parcel containing some of his ashes and the remains of his heart.

# Mary Shelley's Family Tree

Gilbert Imlay [c.1754-1828]

**1.** Married 1797

**2.** Married 1801

Mary Wollstonecraft (1759-1797)
*Died of a fever ten days after daughter Mary's birth.*

William Godwin (1756-1836)
*Died of catarrhal fever.*

Mary Jane Vial Clairmont [c.1766-1841]

Charles Gaulis Clairmont? [c.1766-1796]

Fanny Imlay (1794-1816)
*Later Fanny Godwin. Committed suicide.*

Charles Clairmont (1795-1850)

**1.** Married 1811 (secretly) 1814 (officially)

**2.** Married 1816

Harriet Westbrooke (1795-1816)
*Drowned.*

Percy Bysshe Shelley (1792-1822)
*Drowned in boating accident.*

Mary Wollstonecraft Godwin (1797-1851)
*Later known as Mary Shelley. Died from disease of the brain, supposed tumour.*

William Godwin, Jr. (1803-1832)

Clara Mary Jane Clairmont (1798-1879)
*Known as Jane then Claire Clairmont. (Father unknown)*

Lord Byron (1788-1824)
*Died of a fever.*

Charles (1814-1826)

Ianthe (1813-1876)

Clara Allegra (1817-1822)
*Formerly Alba. Died of typhus.*

Clara? (1815-1815)
*Died at 13 days old.*

William (1816-1819)
*Died possibly from malaria.*

Clara Everina (1817-1818)
*Died of dysentery.*

Percy Florence (1819-1889)

Married 1848

Jane Gibson St John

Key:
Parent of ———
Married ≡≡≡
Relationship with • • • •

*Due to the lack of official records of births, deaths and marriages within this period, the above information is derived from extensive research and is as accurate as possible from the limited sources available.*

# 1816...The Birth of Frankenstein

"How I, then a young girl, came to think of, and to dilate upon, so very hideous an idea?"

The year of 1816 saw crop failure and famine, food riots across Europe following the end of the Napoleonic wars, and a heavy June snow fall in New England. France sentenced Napoleon Bonaparte to permanent exile in St Helena, and the author of *Jane Eyre*, Charlotte Brontë, was born in England.

Eighteen-year-old Mary Wollstonecraft Godwin spent the summer of 1816 with her poet lover Percy Bysshe Shelley and her stepsister Claire Clairmont at Maison Chapuis near Colgny in Geneva, Switzerland. They were there to visit Lord Byron and confirm that he was indeed the father of Claire's unborn child.

The weather was peculiar in 1816 – in fact it became known as "the year without a summer", or "The Poverty Year". Temperatures fluctuated between beautiful summer days and near freezing temperatures within a matter of hours. These unusual conditions were most likely the result of the eruption of Volcano Tambora in Indonesia. Not only temperature variations but also torrential rains and terrifying lightning storms plagued the area, with sunsets being particularly spectacular due to the vast quantities of ash in the air. It was this abnormal weather, coupled with the mood of the group and the wilder aspects of the Swiss landscape, that contributed to the birth of the story of *Frankenstein*.

Due to a particularly violent storm on the night of 16th June 1816, Mary and Percy could not return to Maison Chapuis, and so were invited to spend the night with Lord Byron and John Polidori, Byron's young physician, at Villa Diodati. The group read aloud from *The Fantasmagoriana*, a collection of ghost stories translated from German into French, that they had found in the villa. In one of the stories, a group of travellers entertain each other with tales of supernatural experiences; and this inspired Byron to challenge the group to each write a ghost story.

Shelley wrote an unrecorded story based on his life experiences; Byron wrote only a fragment of a novel; while Polidori is thought to have begun *The Vampyre* at this time (many consider the main character in this story, Lord Ruthven, to be based on Lord Byron). Mary was lost for ideas that evening; but she continued, days after the challenge had finished, determined to produce a suitable story.

In her own words:

"I busied myself to think of a story, – a story to rival those which had excited us to this task. One which would speak to the mysterious fears of our nature, and awaken thrilling horror -- one to make the reader dread to look round, to curdle the blood, and quicken the beatings of the heart. If I did not accomplish these things, my ghost story would be unworthy of its name. I thought and pondered -- vainly. I felt that blank incapability of invention which is the greatest misery of authorship."

Abinger papers, Dep. c. 477, fol. 21r © Bodleian Library, University of Oxford

In the days that followed, Mary remained unable to begin her story:

> "Have you thought of a story? I was asked each morning, and each morning I was forced to reply with a mortifying negative."

During one gathering of the group that summer, they debated the nature of the principle of life, and discussed whether there was any probability of it ever being discovered and communicated. These conversations had a profound effect on Mary. She later wrote that when she went to her bedroom, she had a vision:

> "I saw the pale student of unhallowed arts kneeling beside the thing he had put together. I saw the hideous phantasm of a man stretched out, then, on the working of some powerful engine, show signs of life...His success would terrify the artist; he would rush away...hope that...this thing...would subside into dead matter...he opens his eyes; behold the horrid thing stands at his bedside, opening his curtains..."

Mary had at last found her story, and the monster had his creator.

As you can see from the page opposite, she began by writing the lines that open Volume I Chapter V.:

> "It was on a dreary night of November."

# ...and just as in the story, a monster was born!

> "(Frankenstein) is the most wonderful work to have been written at twenty years of age that I ever heard of. You are now five and twenty. And, most fortunately, you have pursued a course of reading, and cultivated your mind in a manner the most admirably adapted to make you a great successful author. If you cannot be independent, who should be?"
> – William Godwin to Mary Shelley

# Frankenstein Lives!

It is testimony to the dramatic nature of the book and the way that it captured the imaginations of people at the time, that a stage version of *Frankenstein* appeared within five years of its first publication.

On 28th July 1823, *Presumption; or The Fate of Frankenstein*, a play with songs by Richard Brinsley Peake, opened at the English Opera House, and ran for thirty-seven performances. The monster was played by T.P. Cooke; and according to one account, his make-up left him with a

"shrivelled complexion, lips straight and black, and a horrible ghastly grin."

The monster is mute in this first adaptation. This has also been the case in many adaptations since, despite Mary Shelley's creation being tormented, tragic and well-spoken.

An 1823 poster from the English Opera House production of the play entitled *Presumption; or, The Fate of Frankenstein*

Mary Shelley went to see the production on 28th August 1823 and was mostly complementary about it in her letter to her friend Leigh Hunt on 9th September, in which she writes:

"*Frankenstein* had prodigious success as a drama & was about to be repeated for the 23rd night at the English Opera House. The play bill amused me extremely, for in the list of dramatis personæ came, ———— by Mr. T. Cooke: this nameless mode of naming the un {n}ameable is rather good. On Friday Aug. 29th, Jane, my father William & I went to the

theatre to see it. Wallack looked very well as F—he is at the beginning full of hope & expectation—at the end of the 1st Act. The stage represents a room with a staircase leading to F's workshop—he goes to it and you see his light at a small window, through which a frightened servant peeps, who runs off in terror when F. exclaims "It lives!"—Presently F himself rushes in horror & trepidation from the room and while still expressing his agony & terror ———— throws down the door of the laboratory, leaps the staircase & presents his unearthly & monstrous person on the stage. The story is not well managed—but Cooke played ———'s part extremely well—his seeking as it were for support—his trying to grasp at the sounds he heard—all indeed he does was well imagined & executed. I was much amused, & it appeared to excite a breathless eagerness in the audience."

It was well received by the critics, too. This review of the play appeared in a London newspaper the day after the premiere:

*THEATRE, English Opera
London Morning Post:
Tuesday, July 29 & Wednesday, July 30
Review of Presumption; or the
Fate of Frankenstein (1823)*

"A new three act piece, described as 'a romance of a peculiar interest,' was last night produced at this theatre, entitled, *Presumption, or the Fate of Frankenstein.*

The fable represents Frankenstein, a man of great science, to have succeeded in uniting the remains of dead persons, so as to form one being, which he endows with life. He has, however, little reason to exult in the triumph of his art; for the creature thus formed, hideous in aspect, and possessed of prodigious strength, spreads terror, and carries ruin wherever he goes. Though wearing the human form, he is incapable of associating with mankind, to whom he eventually becomes hostile, and having killed the mistress and brother of Frankenstein, he finally vanquishes his mortal creator, and perishes himself beneath a falling avalanche. Such is the outline of the business of a drama more extraordinary in its plan, than remarkable for strength in

its execution. There is something in the piecemeal resurrection effected by Frankenstein, which, instead of creating that awful interest intended to arise from it, gives birth to a feeling of horror. We have not that taste for the monstrous which can enable us to enjoy it in the midst of the most startling absurdities. To Lord BYRON, the late Mr. SHELLEY, and philosophers of that stamp, it might appear a very fine thing to attack the Christian faith from a masked battery, and burlesque the resurrection of the dead, by representing the fragments of departed mortals as starting into existence at the command of a man; but we would prefer the comparatively noble assaults of VOLNEY, VOLTAIRE, and PAINE.

In the first scene in which ——— (so the creature of Frankenstein is indicated in the bills) makes his appearance, the effect is terrific. There are other parts in which a very powerful impression is produced on the spectators, but to have made the most of the idea a greater interest ought early in the drama to have been excited for Frankenstein and the destined victims of the non-descript, and he himself would have been an object of greater attention if speech had been vouchsafed. The efforts to relieve the serious action of the Piece by mirth and music were generally successful, and the labours of Mr. WATSON the composer we often loudly applauded.

The acting was very grand. WALLACK as Frankenstein, displayed great feeling and animation; T.P. COOKE as ——— (or the made up man), was tremendously appalling. The other performers did as much as could be expected in the parts allotted to them, and the piece though it met with some opposition at the close had a large majority in its favour, and was announced for repetition."

Further dramatisations followed in quick succession. On 18th August 1823 *Frankenstein; or, the Demon of Switzerland*, a play by Henry M. Milner, took to the stage at the Royal Coburg Theatre in London. Three other stage versions followed that same year: *Humgumption; or, Dr. Frankenstein and the Hobgoblin of Hoxton, Presumption and the Blue Demon* and *Another Piece of Presumption*, the second play by Peake based on the *Frankenstein* story.

In December 1824, *Frank-in-Steam; or, The Modern Promise to Pay* premiered at the Olympic Theatre; while July 1826 saw the opening at the Royal Coburg Theatre of *The Man and The Monster; or The Fate of Frankenstein*, a further interpretation by Henry M. Milner.

Twenty-three years later in December 1849, *Frankenstein; or, The Model Man*, by William and Robert Brough, opened at the Adelphi Theatre and ran for twenty-six performances.

Interestingly, it is within these early plays that the man and the monster were becoming interchangeable, with writers using *Frankenstein* to describe both the scientist and his creation.

The list of adaptations doesn't end there. Steven Earl Forry, author of *Hideous Progenies: Dramatizations of Frankenstein from Mary Shelley to the Present;* and an authority on this dramatic history, has catalogued almost one hundred dramatic adaptations of *Frankenstein* between 1821 and 1986.

## Frankenstein on Film

The birth of motion pictures opened up further opportunities to present the story visually. The first cinematic version of *Frankenstein* appeared in 1910. It was a one reel silent film produced by Edison Films of New York. Their catalogue of the time proudly proclaimed:

"we have carefully omitted anything in Mrs. Shelley's story which might shock any portion of the audience."

This film was assumed to be lost but amazingly was re-discovered in the 1970s, still in a viewable condition. The second *Frankenstein* film was produced in 1915, titled *Life Without Soul* and directed by Joseph W Smiley. The story is of a doctor who creates a man without a soul. At the end of the film, we find out that the young hero has only dreamed the events of the film, after falling asleep reading Mary Shelley's novel. This film is thought to have been lost.

In 1930, Universal Studios bought the film rights to Peggy Webling's play *Frankenstein: An Adventure in the Macabre*, which had premiered in London in 1927. Bela Lugosi was originally put forward as the actor to play the part of the monster. However, a then obscure English actor, William Henry Pratt, who went by the stage name of Boris Karloff, finally got the part. Karloff's success in *Frankenstein* made him an international star, and the film itself became an instant classic of a new genre - the horror movie.

The Granger Collection, New York. Poster for the 1931 film, *Frankenstein* starring Boris Karloff as the monster.

This lumbering, and (again) mute creature, has perhaps been the most recognisable image of Frankenstein's "monster" since then. The creature's now famous flat head and neck-bolt make-up was created by Universal Studios' make-up artist Jack P. Pierce.

*Frankenstein* earned rave reviews, and was voted one of the films of the year by the New York Times. It made huge amounts of money; the production cost of around $270,000 was dwarfed by the takings of more than $12 million.

In all, over fifty films have been made of the *Frankenstein* story, ranging from horror to drama to comedy, such as the brilliant Mel Brooks' *Young Frankenstein* (1974) starring Gene Wilder and Marty Feldman. Unsurprisingly, interest in the story remains as strong as ever today.

2004 saw the release of a TV film based on the *Frankenstein* trilogy of books by Dean R. Koontz. The story takes place in present day New Orleans, where two detectives are hunting the perpetrator of a series of murders. They are assisted by a mysterious "man", who is in fact the first "creation" of a scientist from many years past, and who has been roaming the earth for hundreds of years, searching for his creator and nemesis. The premise of the film is that Mary Shelley based her own book on the story of this "creation".

In contrast, Hallmark Entertainment's four-part TV mini-series, also released in 2004, has often been cited as the most faithful cinematic telling of Mary Shelley's story to date. This adaptation focuses not only on the action, but also on the development of the characters as the story unfolds. It contains all of the important scenes from the novel - including the narratives by Robert Walton — but has one major deviation from the novel: Victor Frankenstein is seen to use electricity from a thunderstorm to give life to his creature. Although this dramatic cinematic effect has been used by the majority of directors over the years, it doesn't appear in Mary Shelley's book.

It is incredible that a story written nearly two-hundred years ago should still be part of our everyday culture. Although the popularity of the films has helped, it is mainly down to the strength of the original story, dealing as it does with complex themes and issues, that has enabled it to survive through the years; from stage to screen, radio to television; and even now being transformed into this full-colour graphic novel.

# Page Creation

## 1. Script

In order to create two versions of the same book, the story is first adapted into two scripts: Original Text and Quick Text. While the degree of complexity changes for each script, the artwork remains the same for both books.

A page from the script of *Frankenstein* showing the two versions of text.

## 2. Rough Sketch

The artist first creates a rough sketch from the panel directions provided by the scriptwriter. The artist considers many things at this stage, including story pacing, emphasis of certain elements to tell the story in the best way, and even lighting of the scene.

The rough sketch created from the above script.

As you can see here, Declan is using the central action to provide a lighter background to this page, which is in contrast to the dark borders used elsewhere in the book.

## 3. Pencils

The artist and Art Director discuss the rough sketches and agree on any changes that are needed. Once a clear direction is established, the artist creates a pencil drawing of the page.

It is interesting to see the changes made from the rough to the pencil. Note how the first two panels have changed drastically, whereas the third and last panel are unchanged.

The main panel showing the monster being hit by the gun shot was reversed to allow the direction of the shot from the previous panel to continue.

The pencil drawing of page 76.

## 4. Inks

From the pencil sketch, an inked version of the same page is created. Inking is not simply tracing over the pencil sketch; it is the process of using black ink to fill in the shaded areas and to add clarity and cohesion to the "pencils". The "inks" give us the final linework prior to the colouring stage.

The inked image, ready for colouring.

## 5. Colouring

Adding colour really brings the page and its characters to life.

There is far more to the colouring stage than simply replacing the white areas with colour. Some of the linework is replaced with colour (like the red of the shot wound), the light sources are considered for shadows and highlights, and effects added. Finally, the whole page is colour-balanced to the other pages of that scene, and to the overall book.

## 6. Lettering

The final stage is to add the captions, sound effects, and dialogue speech bubbles from the script. These are laid on top of the coloured pages. Two versions of each page are lettered, one for each of the two versions of the book (Original Text and Quick Text).

These are then saved as final artwork pages and compiled into the finished book.

**Original Text**

ISBN:
978-1-906332-15-0

**THE CLASSIC NOVEL
BROUGHT TO LIFE IN FULL COLOUR!**

**Quick Text**

ISBN:
978-1-906332-16-7

**THE FULL STORY IN QUICK MODERN
ENGLISH FOR A FAST-PACED READ!**

# LOOK OUT FOR MORE TITLES
# IN THE CLASSICAL COMICS RANGE

## Jane Eyre:
## The Graphic Novel

Published: 29th September 2008 • 144 Pages • £9.99
• Script Adaptation: Amy Corzine • Artwork: John M. Burns • Letters: Terry Wiley

This Charlotte Brontë classic is brought to vibrant life by artist John M. Burns. His sympathetic treatment of Jane Eyre's life during the 19th century will delight any reader, with its strong emotions and wonderfully rich atmosphere. Travel back to a time of grand mansions contrasted with the severest poverty, and immerse yourself in this fabulous love story.

ISBN: 978-1-906332-06-8

ISBN: 978-1-906332-08-2

## A Christmas Carol:
## The Graphic Novel

Published: 13th October 2008 • 160 Pages • £9.99
• Script Adaptation: Sean Michael Wilson • Pencils: Mike Collins
• Inks: David Roach • Colours: James Offredi • Letters: Terry Wiley

A full-colour graphic novel adaptation of the much-loved Christmas story from the great Charles Dickens. Set in Victorian England and highlighting the social injustice of the time, we see one Ebenezer Scrooge go from oppressor to benefactor when he gets a rude awakening to how his life is, and how it should be. With sumptuous artwork and wonderful characters, this magical tale is a must-have for the festive season.

ISBN: 978-1-906332-17-4

ISBN: 978-1-906332-18-1

## OTHER CLASSICAL COMICS TITLES:

**Great Expectations**
Published: January 2009
Original Text    978-1-906332-09-9
Quick Text    978-1-906332-11-2

**Romeo & Juliet**
Published: July 2009
Original Text    978-1-906332-19-8
Plain Text    978-1-906332-20-4
Quick Text    978-1-906332-21-1

**Richard III**
Published: March 2009
Original Text    978-1-906332-22-8
Plain Text    978-1-906332-23-5
Quick Text    978-1-906332-24-2

**Dracula**
Published: September 2009
Original Text    978-1-906332-25-9
Quick Text    978-1-906332-26-6

**The Tempest**
Published: May 2009
Original Text    978-1-906332-29-7
Plain Text    978-1-906332-30-3
Quick Text    978-1-906332-31-0

**The Canterville Ghost**
Published: October 2009
Original Text    978-1-906332-27-3
Quick Text    978-1-906332-28-0

For more information visit www.classicalcomics.com

# TEACHERS' RESOURCES

To accompany each title in our series of graphic novels, we also publish a set of teachers' resources. These widely acclaimed photocopiable books are designed by teachers, for teachers, to help meet the requirements of the UK curriculum guidelines. Aimed at upper Key Stage 2 and above, each book provides exercises that cover structure, listening, understanding, motivation and comprehension as well as key words, themes and literary techniques. Although the majority of the tasks focus on the use of language in order to align with the revised framework for teaching English, you will also find many cross-curriculum topics, covering areas within history, ICT, drama, reading, speaking, writing and art; and with a range of skill levels, they provide many opportunities for differentiated teaching and the tailoring of lessons to meet individual needs.

*Classical Comics Study Guide: Frankenstein*
Black and white, spiral bound A4 (making it easy to photocopy).

Price: £19.99
ISBN: 978-1-906332-37-2

Published: October 2008

## DIFFERENTIATED TEACHING AT YOUR FINGERTIPS!

"Because the exercises feature illustrations from the graphic novel, they provide an immediate link for students between the book and the exercise – however they can also be used in conjunction with any traditional text; and many of the activities can be used completely stand-alone. I think the guide is fantastic and I look forward to using it. I know it will be a great help and lead to engaging lessons . It is easy to use, another major asset. Seriously: well done, well done, well done!"

*Kornel Kossuth,*
*Head of English, Head of General Studies*

"Thank you! These will be fantastic for all our students. It is a brilliant resource and to have the lesson ideas too are great. Thanks again to all your team who have created these."

*B.P. KS3*

"Thank you so much. I can't tell you what a help it will be."
*A very grateful teacher, Kerryann SA*

- "you've certainly got a corner of East Anglia convinced that this is a fantastic way to teach and progress English literature and language!!"
*Chris Mehew*

"With many thanks again for your excellent resources and upbeat philosophy."

*Dr. Marcella McCarthy*
*Leading Teacher for Gifted and Talented Education,*
*The Cherwell School, Oxford*

"Dear Classical Comics,
Can I just say a quick "thank you" for the excellent teachers' resources that accompanied the *Henry V* Classical Comics. I needed to look no further for ideas to stimulate my class. The children responded with such enthusiasm to the different formats for worksheets, it kept their interest and I was able to find appropriate challenges for all abilities. The book itself was read avidly by even the most reluctant readers. Well done, I'm looking forward to seeing the new titles."

*A. Dawes, Tockington Manor School*

"I wanted to write to thank you - I had a bottom set Y9 class that would have really struggled with the text if it wasn't for your comics, THANK YOU."

*Dan Woodhouse*

"As to the resource, I can't wait to start using it! Well done on a fantastic service."
*Will*

## OUR RANGE OF OTHER CLASSICAL COMICS STUDY GUIDES

| *Henry V* | *Macbeth* | *Jane Eyre* | *A Christmas Carol* | *Great Expectations* |
|---|---|---|---|---|
| Published: November 2007 | Published: March 2008 | Published: October 2008 | Published: October 2008 | Published: January 2009 |
| Price: £19.99 | Price: £19.99 | Price: £19.99 | Price: £19.99 | Price: £19.99 |
| ISBN: 978-1-906332-07-5 | ISBN: 978-1-906332-10-5 | ISBN: 978-1-906332-12-9 | ISBN: 978-1-906332-38-9 | ISBN: 978-1-906332-13-6 |

# BRINGING CLASSICS TO COMIC LIFE

Classical Comics has partnered with Comic Life to bring you a unique comic creation experience!

Comic Life is an award-winning software system that is used and loved by millions of children, adults and schools around the world. The software allows you to create astounding comics in a matter of minutes – and it is really easy and fun to use, too!

Through RM Distribution, you can now obtain all of our titles in every text version, electronically for use with any computer or whiteboard system. In addition, you can also obtain our titles as "No Text" versions that feature just the beautiful artwork without any speech bubbles or captions. These files can then be used in Comic Life (or any other

software that can handle jpg files) enabling anyone to create their own version of one of our famous titles.

All of the digital versions of our titles are available from RM on a single user or site-license basis.

For more details, visit www.rm.com and search for Classical Comics, or visit www.classicalcomics.com / education.

### Classical Comics, RM and Comic Life - Bringing Classics to Comic Life!